MERCY

Also by Shirley Camia
The Significance of Moths

Mercy

Shirley Camia

TURNSTONE PRESS

Turnstone Press
Artspace Building
206-100 Arthur Street
Winnipeg, MB
R3B 1H3 Canada
www.TurnstonePress.com

Turnstone Press gratefully acknowledges the assistance of the Canada Council for the Arts, the Manitoba Arts Council, the Government of Canada, and the Province of Manitoba through the Book Publishing Tax Credit and the Book Publisher Marketing Assistance Program.

Original hand-sculpted glass candy on cover by Kevin McKay.

Printed and bound in Canada.

Library and Archives Canada Cataloguing in Publication

Title: Mercy / Shirley Camia.
Names: Camia, Shirley, author.
Description: Poems.
Identifiers: Canadiana (print) 20189067659 | Canadiana (ebook) 20189067667 | ISBN 9780888016614 (softcover) | ISBN 9780888016621 (EPUB) | ISBN 9780888016638 (Kindle) | ISBN 9780888016645 (PDF)
Classification: LCC PS8605.A49 M47 2019 | DDC C811/.6—dc23

For Mom

Contents

Memento

Completing the Crossing

MERCY

Dream I

you are headed
for another long
journey

moving

through an exit
marked the past
that meets the future

and the pilot
is calling
your name

all you take
is a suitcase
brimming

with
sunflowers

(they follow every movement of the sun)

yellow
leaves a silent
goodbye

as you walk

without looking
back

sombre as
night

Dusk

Blizzard

a cruel
january storm

rushes in
on a clipped wing

covers the plain
like a sheet

Because It's Hard to Hear the Truth, Part 1

your stare
hides oceans
when you say

this isn't going to change

of course it will
just do what the doctor says
and everything will be alright

your chest falls
aches

like mourning

a promise
soon
broken

Body

there in your bed
lies an atlas

an archipelago of bones

ridges and valleys
of sunken flesh

estuaries of veins

but

under the blankets
of clothes

a beating heart

Hidden Message

you say
i'm losing my looks

and unrepentant explain
looks are fleeting

perhaps this is a way to distance yourself
to mark your stop on the road

because it's easier to say than what's really there

under the hospital stays
the soft food

the tubes
on your face

like a wreath

you're losing your mother

Because It's Hard to Hear the Truth, Part 2

after the doctor
delivers the news

your fingers curl
to cradle themselves

after the doctor
delivers the news

you hum yourself
a lullaby

after the doctor
delivers the news

you lower your head
and say nothing

after the doctor
delivers the news

you bite your lip
and draw blood

your breath in a cage

Feeding the Wolves

how long do i have

a question i can't answer
a question that howls
a question that travels in a pack

how did this happen
why
did i do enough
did i do it right
where will i go
when did i get so old

And Then You Console Me

the strokes of your hand
are heavy against my head

your fingers
pulling at strands

but i keep still

avoiding the charts

the clock
and its steady dirge

the nurses
who watch

Dusk

when the day
surrenders

when all is dark

when you join
a constellation
of stars

and crown
the frozen night

In Our Last Moment Alone

the only things i can do

fix your crooked barrette
smooth your rumpled cover
bend my cheek to yours

A New Ritual

just one cup of coffee

tatay says to the cashier

as he's wrapped in your old
winter coat

it's the colour of lilacs

and the circles pleading
under his eyes

just one cup of coffee

no
no more donut

yes only one coffee

one

Dream II

this is our new life now
we have to make do
and learn how to take it from here

ok mom
how

you turn away
(lost to me again)

vanish

Morning 1

we drive by
our old house

where the white paint fades

and the yellow underneath
is starting to bleed through

the plum tree chopped
the blossoms long withered

the one-car garage
turned into two

your polyester curtains

hang like shadows
in the windows

thick enough to hide
the visitors in our home

making it their own

Morning 2

at your apartment

~

adobo and pancit
a memory
on the burners

cigarettes have taken over the rooms

~

your avocado shake
is still in the freezer

all there but a few sips

What I Will Never Know

did you see the arches
fall to a line

did you hear the beeps
collide

were you ready
did you cry

were you scared

was it dark
or full of light

did you see lola

can you breathe

What People Say at a Wake

Dream III

i chant

sorry
sorry
sorry

to a wilted
weeping buddha

sorry
as you crumble

into

dust

Novena

on the very first day

the aunts
are lighting candles

in front
of a grainy photo

of you

in the philippines
at an empty buffet

(smiling
an unnatural smile)

their prayers fill the room

aba ginoong maria
napupuno ka ng grasiya

outside the snow
is rampant

battered

santa maria ina ng diyos

all i can think
they made us take your clothes

at kung kami'y mamamatay

you must be so cold

On the Third Day

the back gate swings

three knocks
on the door inside

your scent drifts

a baby laughs
cries

What People Say at a Wake

condolence
condolences

she looks like she's sleeping
she lost so much weight

which one is her daughter
she was my best friend

i dare you to touch her
i can't even look

i'm sorry
so sorry

goodbye
and goodbye

and goodbye

The Resounding Drone of a Eulogy (in a Minor Key)

my voice
is a squawky
horn

that fails at jokes
at your funeral

my voice
is a squawky
horn

that stumbles over
sentences
and trips

on awkward
pauses

my voice
is a squawky
horn

that struggles
to find
the right tones

Despedida

do you see
your freshly coloured hair

and the lace you wore to that wedding
just over a year before

it hangs so differently
on the body in front of me now

your face is changed
in a mysterious way

transformed
without its spirit

i put candy in your hands

under the broken rosary
weaving through your fingers

like ivy

because you never know
who you're going to meet

Procession

even a stranger

forms the sign of the cross
for you

as we pass

his sigh
sent skyward

the way your soul
gracefully departed

your body

cruising through lights
leading the way

Interment

there is a scream
but it's silent

as it falls six feet

landing on your
casket with a thud

under the white drifts

and the scattered
purple petals

torn leaves

severed stems

As You Wish

you are still in the philippines

by a dock inhaling sea salt
enjoying the dance of the palms

your ancestral home

of your nieces and nephews
sisters and brothers
mother and father

above and below the earth

where the taste of milkfish
is clean and pure

where you are full
of mangoes and youth

in a time that eclipses all meaning

you are still in the philippines

but you're buried in snow
an ocean away

at your request

Dream IV

LIGHTS UP
CUE APPLAUSE

the audience claps
at a blinking sign

LIGHTS OUT
APPLAUSE OUT

before darkness
forces a hush

before darkness
is sliced

SPOTLIGHT UP

by a tenuous
streak of light

CUE

and you come

act 1

then the tsunami

Sorting through Documents at Dawn

three crosses appear
on the tv screen

following a
sweep of my hair

that felt like your hand

maybe i dreamt it
but i so badly

want it to be you
(in whatever form)

near

not in the light through
which you've disappeared

leaving us
with questions

what is your social insurance number
what is your mother's maiden name

how

who am i now

(and in between
the writing
found

on perfectly pressed
pages

a comma
and a curse

who were you)

It's All Just Stuff (but)

what i couldn't touch before
i throw out

coffee cups
cough drops
faded receipts
bills
styrofoam
plastic
newspapers
foil

what i can't throw out now
i keep

marriage certificate
wedding dress
pictures
gifts
cards
a ticket to a broadway show
a hospital bracelet that says your name and baby
592322

The Subtle Wail of Spring

a life
reduced to boxes

a life
replaced by an estate

a hole
in empty space

and yet

the buds bloom
the days return
the sparrows call

only the jagged ends
of icicles

soften
into teardrops

(the snow is meeting its own quiet end)

MEMENTO

Dream V

ME

(Looking at you.)

what happened
to the fancy blouse
and the lilac skirt
you wore last

(Pointing to your clothes. Beat.)

why the stained blue shirt
and the big floral shorts
you died in

YOU

(Beat. Exiting.)

i only wear nice clothes to parties

(You exit. Blackout.)

A Memory on the Burners

in the pot of
polished silver

blackened scabs
trace an outline

of a woman

it's really easy
just take short ribs

(ask the butcher to cut them)

boil them in water
drain
then
add water
mix garlic
and pepper
soy sauce and vinegar
and a bayleaf
boil again

that's it

that's it

The Unstoppable Rumble

i can't control what happens

over dinner
under sunlight
or in the middle of the street

when i remember

all there is
is sadness

a hollow encased in flesh

How Things Change

i once wished
for visits to the mall

not trips to the hospital
on different floors

in disbelief
that aging

(your aging)

was real

and fumbling its way
towards death

now i wish for those inpatient days

of ailments and worries
vials and cartoons

and a mother

Queen

remember that time

i sat in your lap
hair matted to my face

damp from the sweat
of child's play

cousins swarmed like frantic bees
a nest of sticky limbs

you were the eye

what I've Learned

time isn't measured by age

it's marked
by days
with you

and all the things that follow

all that is uncertain
all that i never asked you
all that i wasn't ready to
all that i had no need to
all that is important to me

now

Memento

your umbrella smells of perpetual dusk

after a lunch of fried rice and salad rolls
pushcart mazes in grocery stores
a change of clothes
and a click of the remote

sunset cut in slivers
shreds on the wall

a summer day
in nylon
pressed hard against my nose

looks from wet strangers passing

Everything Makes Sense Looking Back

it was the end
when you forgot my birthday

(i should have known)

the day i was ripped
from your stomach

and you were sewn
with crude stitches

(scars plotting map routes
in your flesh)

is it wednesday today

no i said staring at the pale peach walls
blocks from where i was born

it's monday

Easter

the night extinguishes itself
on the day of the resurrection

a ceremony marked

by the clutch of hymns
and a jubilant organ

a chorus
with one less voice

Morning 47

our last words
our last words

our last words

i'm dizzy from them
repeating themselves

spinning
like a ride at a playground

(you know the one)

the one with the shiny bars
that blind
and burn
at the touch

but i

(as you've
warned me before)

hold on tight

You Learning a New Language
Is Not Entirely Unlike Me Grieving

confusing

f and p
he and she

opening/closing vs. turning on/off the light

on and in
they're/their/there

singular and plural
present and past

Scavenger Hunt

i look for you everywhere
in any and all places

bus stops
parked cars
the backs of strangers' heads

(it could be you
it could really be you)

you come to me in fragments

a line in a script
a note in a chord

pieces that summon a whole
(hole)

treasure

A Short-Lived Visit

under a tarnished coin
of a full moon

your fragrance
is caught

in a gasp
of grey mist

it flees
like geese

at the perch
of the first cold

dots in the sky
fireworks in reverse

Autodial

this morning
when i woke
i thought

i'm just being dramatic

i almost called you
to apologize

for the fiction of these poems

A Year of Questions and I Don't Knows

that itchy pink gown
still hangs in the closet

the one in which
you held me

under the gaze of god

a prayer of mercy
for the trail of hopes

ahead

did i detour
(yes)

do i make you proud

Completing the Crossing

Dream VI

a door opens and shuts
three times

and you say my name
the way only you do

where are you

behind the door you say

a silhouette moves
in the crack of the frame

(white light
and a tv screen appears)

you

(in clothes i don't know)

a lavender blazer
hair cut and coloured

healthy
young

you say the things
you never got to say

a flash
of violet smoke

and you're gone

Completing the Crossing

a roar leads a tail of smoke
then we're off

back to your home

charging through water

so dirty
so deep

we could drown

You Are Here

in the drooping belt
on a crooked hook

in the pillows and sheets
dressing unmade beds

in the duster gathering
dust on the floor

in the quiet
of an empty chair

in the parts of faces
resembling yours

in the town
where you were born

Home

around the back of the house
past the narrow path
is the sea

and it carries you with it

until you reach the point where the sky
and the swell collapse into one

a flight of the birds marks your return

Intersections

i remember all that is lost
when the roosters crow

the puppies squirm
the chatter stops

the door bangs shut
the house is still

except the ghosts

Lapida

we visit you on mother's day
the ground above you

flat (like the world was once believed)

waiting for sod
and your name

to mark your new address

and when that comes
i can no longer

deny

what's been hard to believe
and impossible to say

you are dead

Mercy

a two year old smiles

at a shadow
only he sees

unaware

of the separation
between the anguished

and a lightness in the air

sorrow's shell cracked
open with laughter

mercy in a christmas cactus

blooming
in july

Always Remembered, Always Loved

it's the end of the summer
and a breeze has blown

dust
onto your grave

so i tidy

dividing necessity
from clutter

flowers
from withered petals

only to find it

nestled there
in the stems

a moth

resting
quietly

a spirit

separate
from the body

keeping vigil

Notes

Page 3—Dream I
"Like a Sunflower" is a Christian hymn.

Page 24—Novena
The lines in Tagalog are part of the prayer, "Hail Mary."

Page 69—Alway Remembered, Always Loved
There is a Filipino superstition that a person who has passed away visits loved ones in the form of a moth.

Glossary

Adobo—A popular dish in which meat is marinated and cooked in vinegar, soy sauce, and garlic.

Despedida—A farewell (derived from Spanish); a send-off party for one about to embark on a journey.

Lapida—Spanish in origin, lapida is the Filipino term for gravestone.

Lola—Derived from the Spanish word abuela, lola is a common term for grandmother in the Philippines.

Pancit—A Filipino noodle dish.

Tatay—The Tagalog word for father.

Acknowledgements

Earlier versions of some of these poems were published in *The New Quarterly* ("Body," "Memento," and "Despedida"), *CV2* ("As You Wish"), *TAYO* ("Novena," "Interment," "Queen," and "Body"), and *My Lot Is A Sky* ("Always Remembered, Always Loved" published as "Always a Mother," Math Paper Press, 2018).

My deep gratitude to Jamis Paulson, Sharon Caseburg, Melissa McIvor, and Sarah Ens with Turnstone Press for their continued faith in my work.

To the authors whose works I devoured in the months following my mother's death and whose influences are found in these poems:
Margaret Atwood
Billy Collins
Dennis Cooley
Hope Edelman
Gail Eisenberg
Diane Hambrook
Janice Lee
Tanis MacDonald
Hoa Nguyen
Meghan O'Rourke
Mary Oliver
Michael Ondaatje
Aimee Suzara
Wisława Szymborska
Priscila Uppal

Thank you to Robert Joseph for the ever-critical eye.

To my family and friends for their encouragement and support.

Love to Andy. Always.